Notes / Examples

Amazing Magical adventures of Poppy Flower– (A short story from my dreams and imagination starting on 7/20/2004)

Author: Vicki Rae Thomas

This is my imagination and dreams written down for all to read and enjoy.

Thank you, to my husband Bob for believing in me.

My dreams and story start with Poppy Flower. Clearly Poppy was not like other people. She is one of a few nature dwellers called Liveling's. They live in a vast forest area hidden away from human civilization and in a desolate remote area. Most hard core rock climbers or adventurers would not even think of venturing anywhere close. Poppy is adventurous and she wants to experience real adventures first hand verses being told stories passed down from generation to generation. A generation is a very long time since the Liveling's as they are known, live for centuries. You would not know it by looking at Poppy, but she is 150 years old. Her outward appearance looks like she is about twenty. It is a combination of no stress and the Liveling's magical lineage. They are a cross between elf and fairy.

Their bodies are very beautiful and they have proportionate anatomy. No outward signs like elongated or pointed ears. No wings or other appendages. Their skin is light. Female hair varies in shades and colors, from black to blonde and even rainbow colors. They have shoulder length hair that looks like it is floating. Male hair styles are straight to curly. The Males have thick hair and have short bob type cut. There is never a need to cut their hair. It is always perfect. No split ends, frizz or bald spots. Hair that looks as if it was just cut, colored and styled.

Livelings have a pixie like quality because they are small and petite. The average height is about 3-5 foot tall. If they were in the human civilized world they would be mistaken for human Little People. The Liveling's pride themselves with being well organized and knowledgeable, especially when it comes to the forest. All the animals and plants that they are in contact with, they protect and care for. The Liveling's respect their elders who live for centuries. The only way a Liveling can die is only by an accident. Never old age. Longevity is in their genes. Some elders are so old that when asked, they just say "I quit counting at Five Hundred". No one really knows how old the elders are. How old is the forest? It boggles your mind. Liveling's don't show normal signs of aging. No wrinkles, hunching over, limping or the need to walk with a cane. No gray hair, they just look young forever. There is no real change after 20 years old. Most males like her father Snap Dragon have extraordinary strength even when they are hundreds of years old. They never get sick and when they hurt themselves or brake any body parts, with their awesome self-healing powers, they recovery almost overnight. The only way to die is to be decapitated or eaten. Their healing power cannot function with their mind, body, or major organs being separated. (An important part of the healing and telepathic process). This does not happen very often. When their body and mind are separated, their ethereal ability to heal ceases to exist. Only freak accidents like the rare encounter of say a large wild animal. That animal might react too quickly or they were not familiar with the friendly Liveling's. Possibly before the telepathy kicked in. This is so rare that the Livelings never really think about it. There is only folk lore and stories about this at the fire pit get together.

Back to Poppy and her appearance. She is a red head with yellow and orange highlights. It looks like her head is on fire when she is dancing or running on a windy day. The movement seems almost as if it is in slow motion. Her eyes are a light aqua blue and are like looking into a shallow pond. They have a sparkle like diamonds dancing on the water when the sun hits the water just right. It is mesmerizing to look into her eyes. A Liveling has perfect sight. You never see one with glasses, even when they are centuries old. They all have rosy checks and lips that look like they just put on makeup. It makes sense since they are magical beings. Liveling's have exceptional skin. No blemishes, discoloration or wrinkles. It is as if they are locked in time.

They are a small clan with telepathic abilities, longevity and endless experiences according to their stories at the fire pit and the passing down of information. Truth is Liveling's usually do not use their astral projecting ability anymore. They have mostly forgotten it. Poppy was however intrigued by the stories. Especially when she learned there are a few forgotten clans. The Flower family are distant cousins to the Fir and Pine Clans. Some are positive like the Livelings. Other clans are negative and some are even evil. More on these other clans later.

A little background on Poppy Flower's parents. Snap Dragon Flower (Father) has blonde hair like all Liveling males. He has red tipped patches in a checker board pattern. It is an unusual pattern but the fire red looked good with the blonde. All clans are enchanted folk. Most, but not all females in Poppy's family have varying shades of red, thick hair and teal blue eyes. Poppy has some freckles, which give her a pixie like appearance. I think she got those freckles from her father. His whole face is covered with freckles. He is also very muscular and strong. Liveling males can carry 10-50 times their weight, like ants. Snap Dragon is at the 50 times level. It is an impressive magical sight to see, when he is carrying a huge rock or moving a tree stump as if it was a light piece of furniture.

Daisy Flower is Poppy's mother and she has reddish maroon colored hair with a dark purple streak in the front that flows down the right side of her face. She is very beautiful and more sultry looking than Poppy. One of Poppy's similar traits to her mother is her floating hair look. Daisy only has a few freckles. Her body type is more voluptuous and curvy. Poppy is very athletic and has a more stream lined look. Daisy is much more reserved in her demeanor and she does not like taking risks. She has a great love for the plants and animals. Daisy will go out of her way to help a baby bird that falls out of a tree or a fox that is injured. She is the Liveling healer who set up and runs the nature clinic.

Poppy is the first in a very long, long time to venture outside of the Liveling valley boundaries. These boundaries are hidden by a vast forest that blends into an unforgiving snow covered, rocky mountain range, with smooth sheer glacier cliffs. Both, completely unpassable. This is where they have lived for hundreds of years, in peace and harmony along with nature. When Poppy was exploring she found this cave of secret doors, by accident. She was walking with her hand gliding along a smooth rock and her hand disappeared. She pulled it back quickly and that was the start of her adventures with the Cave of Never Ending Doors. Poppy came to understand why safety usually depends on life and death decisions. Procedures should always be followed, even though many doors are very positive. You never know when something might change or be effected by evil.

When Poppy visits the vast number of secret doors she found it was necessary to create an access portal door that leads to her room in her Liveling's family home. She does not spend much time in this room. It is more of a walk through space. She secretly spends most of her time exploring the Cave of Never Ending Doors, where she found out not all doors are friendly, happy doors. She realized the need to be careful and mark the doors that she has already explored with descriptive markings so she would know quickly whether it was a good experience or a not. These markings will be explained later. She has not come across a door or room she could not handle. What holds her fascination is the not knowing what is on the other side of a door. She does get some assistance from her dragon friend, Sordo. More detail on Sordo later. As Poppy walks past some of the heavy oversized doors made of wood with large metal latches. These bulky doors, chains, multi locks and sturdy bolts are designed to keep others out and were created centuries ago. These doors and security can last until the end of time. Designed to protect what is behind the doors. Her safety usually depends on how the doors looked or her interaction with them. Safety has a lot to do with how she telepathic feelings about when the door was created and who the architects were. Some doors have so many different locks on them it would take a Locksmith Wizard to unlock them. Poppy usually stays away from the doors with heavy ominous looking locks.

There is a key room. Poppy has seen this centuries old room. It is not well organized and has millions of keys inside, with every shape, size, color and some keys even use musical tones. They play a note or notes to open the doors. This room is the size of a large warehouse. Cabinets and shelves full of boxes and containers. It would take someone a lifetime to even sort the keys. Then another lifetime to match all the keys with the appropriate doors. Most of the doors she explores are open and do not require a key, making it easier since Poppy believes the key list has been lost or misplaced by a waring clan member centuries ago. The list could have been magically sealed with a spell rendering it invisible, making the list impossible to locate. Now only the stories are left from centuries of forbidden and forgotten doors. These stories are passed on and told to the Younling's during the fire pit get together (a Youngling is a Liveling, less than fifty years old). They stories were added to and enhanced for climactic endings.

Poppy's clan lives hidden and protected inside a very treacherous mountain range, sheer cliffs and a narrow ice path. This path is where most outside explorers would fall to their death. Into deep crevices that appear to have no bottom. Most would call it, unforgiving and unpassable. This mountain range that leads to the Liveling's valley has high cliffs with flat rock-faces thousands of feet high that snow does not even gather on. Rarely would this endeavor be challenged even by the best and most elite rock climbers. Similar to the dangerous atmosphere of Mount Everest. Think of the invisible Shangri La in those old movies, where anyone who tried to get to Shangri La would endure unforgiving blizzards. Most would die horribly by freezing to death on the narrow icy path. Only an elite special few would make it to the very thin almost invisible cut in the mountain. Finding it only when standing just exactly in the right spot. If they were even one inch off the entrance would never reveal itself and they would die of exposure. Very rarely did anyone continue on from the unforgiving path. The rare few who saw it, went on through the tunnel pass to the other end, opening up to a lush warm valley paradise. No pyramid of solid gold in the center, but a sun shining. There are birds singing, butterflies fluttering in sprawling green tree canopies. A gorgeous warm valley full of flowers. This is the perilous path to the Liveling's Valley paradise. The Livelings homes and buildings are carved into the mountainside. More spectacular than any known Indian mountain dwellings.

Poppy being agile physically, could not have managed this feat if not for her special ability. A rare gift of being able to physically project herself to another place by the power of thought. Ancient Livelings could astral project. That is how in the past they learned about the rest of the world. The majority could only visualize and could not physically experience it. After hearing so many stories of other Liveling experiences, Poppy tried to astral project herself. She realized that she was able to do both physical and astral projection. She was so excited after her first teleporting experience. It was more exhilarating than her astral projecting. She immediately knew the difference because she was able to feel the wind, smell the flowers and feel the dirt or sand under her feet. This could be very dangerous for her clan. It posed a problem of discovery for the Livelings and the possibility of exposure and their way of life. Even their very existence. She has to be very careful not to expose her secret. For Poppy, it opened up a whole new world of adventures in addition to the Cave of Doors. There are many treasures beyond anyone's wildest dreams in the Cave of Never Ending Doors and Worlds. Enough adventures for multiple life times. Exploration and magic combined. These doors and the knowledge of them was hidden from the Liveling's a long time ago. Problems in the past were from one Liveling coming very close to being discovered by humans or other clans. This careless Liveling did not follow the rules. He was observed popping in and out, with his reckless astral projection and teleporting capability. His name was Fern. Some enlightened humans are able to see an aura or ghost like image of someone when they astral project. Fern was a Youngling Stories of this event tell how this event was almost the demise of the Liveling civilization. A story of humans becoming curious and obsessed with the idea of finding out the secret of this one Liveling Fern Wood, of the Fir Clan. He was adventurous like Poppy but he took way to many risks. Fern was always Astral Projecting and transporting to the same place all the time and not going to different areas. That was the reason he was noticed. The place he originally transported to by accident was easy and quite frankly the only place his capabilities allowed him to go. He liked it because it was simple. Fern was lazy, unorganized and did not always follow the rules. He found out in the end, that safety and being careful is very important and to always follow the rules or there are consequences. Fern was always the bad character in most of the stories passed down from generation to generation. This story happened a couple hundred years ago, when Poppy was not even a sparkle in her father's eye.

Ferns story starts with him venturing outside of the Liveling and Fir Clans mountainous area one day, quite by accident. The two clans used to share this valley. After Fern's and the Fir Clans disgrace of revealing both clans to possible annihilation. The Fir Clan left after pressure from the Livelings (Back to the story) Fern was astral projecting. All clans had this ability. When all of a sudden he was physically transported to a desolate area, similar in comparison to the Sahara desert. This area had large sand dunes, no vegetation and the temperature was at or above 100 degrees. Fern was startled by what had just happened and as soon as he got to the desert. He was immediately transported back. Fern tried again and again after that. Not that he enjoyed the sand dunes or the heat but that he actually physically transported back to this desert area. It was a feat in itself. Poppy called it teleporting (so that is how it will be addressed from now on). Fern was unsuccessful in trying to duplicate this most of the time, but he kept trying. On occasion he would teleport there. Finally he had it fine tuned and he could teleport there as often as he wanted. But only to that exact spot and time. No matter how hard he tried he was unable to teleport any where else. Unaware, he was being observed, by a clan of Nomads. They were at a desert oasis close by and hidden by magic. Fern was exposed. He was able to astral project to other spots but it was not enough and he got bored. He had overheard conversations from others in the clan about a cave and when he hunted for and found the cave, he spent more time exploring the Cave of Never Ending Doors and abandoned trying to teleport. It was too late though his secret was out and spreading like wild fire. The Liveling Clan had no choice. The Fir Clan was asked to leave and was relocated by the Liveling Clan Elders centuries ago.

Poppy had the true gift. Most Liveling's did not have the teleporting capability. They were only able to astral project. Just a rare few in the long Liveling line in history were said to possess this ability. That is where it gets tricky. Fern did not have the control or the accuracy that Poppy does. She can pin point the exact spot as easily as walking to it, just by visualizing where and when. Down to the exact inch and minute. Fern was not so lucky with his control or accuracy. He could not even hit a different area or time. This effected both clans safety. Anyway that is how the story goes. Even when he tried to vary his location or time. If he was not careful he might end up in the dark ages. He decided to only venture into doors he had explored before. Fern was too late and was unprepared for what happened and it lead to his death. One of the stories told says he ended up with evil beings in a world and possibly got eaten by a large dinosaur type creature. This happened when he could not concentrate and was unable to find the exit while running for his life. Since no one was with him, there are multiple and varying stories of what actually happened to him. Story tellers had to piece together information given to Ferns friends. Fern always told his friends stories of where he had been, what he had seen and experienced. Fern loved the attention and would always embellish his stories. So when it came to his actual demise, all they had was his stories. Extreme folk tales mixed with extreme reality. That was always Poppy's favorite version of the story. Wild accusations of doors with worlds filled with absurd creatures and harsh surroundings. Like the story Fern told his friends about his first experience. It was of an upside down world. Where he walked on the clouds in the blue sky. Remembering that when he looked up at the ground it had a running brook, flowers and rocks. Strange creature type animals walking on the ground, but overhead. Many of these creature animals were similar to Elk and had large antlers, but they had shorter legs. He said they would jump and ended up back on the upside down ground. Fish swimming in the water overhead, that did not fall out or birds flying by him upside down. Fern said he only had a brief encounter with this world. He said it felt like he would fall into the sky that he was standing on. A very confusing world behind the Upside Down World Door. The door was easy to identify because of the picture of the sky on the bottom and ground with flowers on the top. Fern said it was very hard on his equilibrium to be in that world. He may have been uncomfortable, but he was always intrigued by this unique door-world. It was thought that he may have gone into this world for the last time and no one heard from him again. Another story of his last adventure was where he possibly tried to conquer his discomfort. There are other stories. Really there is no way of knowing for sure, which story is true, since his friends embellished all stories of his death? Poppy opened the door once but did not step through. She wanted to wait until she had a plan first.

Poppy became very proficient at teleporting herself back and forth between her homes in the human world and the Liveling picturesque but simpler world, while trying not to let either world know about her secrets. She rarely used the family/human door. She only set it up in case she ever had a problem teleporting. She would be able to walk into this parlor style room. It was created for privacy and if she needed to teleport secretly. This way she had a backup plan (more on this later). The Liveling cave door that she created has a picture of the Liveling high, sharp, mountain peaks on one side and her human house pictured on the other side. Using subtle colors on this door. It was a pleasure to view and admire as she walked by. The door looked like a beautiful painting as a majority of the doors did. She could see the masterful trim work detail of her house and the beautiful meadow flowers of the entry point past the mountain cut and on the other side of the entrance. A depiction of the treacherous journey that was laid out earlier. Poppy only had to think of what she wanted as decoration on the doors and it would just manifest, exactly as she saw it in her mind.

The Liveling's are simple folk living magical lives. They are very healthy and their physical bodies do not deteriorate like the humans fragile bodies. Livelings have the power to heal themselves, animals, plants and other life forces in the forest. They live in a symbiotic relationship and they all help one another. Liveling's can telepathically communicate with the forest plants, trees and animals. Liveling's are vegetarians and praise the food as they eat it. All the vegetables they grow are used for food that feeds themselves and the animals. All the vegetables and fruits they farm are completely consumed. They plant the seeds that are growing on the vine because there are no seeds inside the fruits or vegetables. Nothing is done without a purpose or meaning. It is like a perfect Fairy Tale.

Poppy wanted change in her life. She was bored with her life the way it was. So one day she ventured in to the human world by accidentally astral projecting and then teleported to that spot. After countless times back and forth from the human world, she came to the conclusion she would purchase a house in the suburbs. This would make it easier for her to experience human behavior without being detected. The house is also a gateway to the Cave of Never Ending Doors and a way to keep the Liveling secret. She has done a lot of investigation of the options and how best to put her plan together without bringing unnecessary attention to her and her kind. She is very aware of the dangers because of the old folk tales she has heard growing up her entire life. She likes to experiment with visits to different types of sites by astral projection. To and from hot unforgiving deserts and to the coldest ice caves in the North Pole. She did not return to those locations physically for obvious reasons. She has dabbled with going to the sky scrapers of New York, Tokyo and to the Australian Outback. She has no restrictions of where she can go as long as she can imagine it. She has even by astral means visited Mars and the Moon. She abandoned going to any other planets since they are boring and have no life at all. She usually goes somewhere by astral projection first and only when she knows she can teleport safely, she will. Poppy has visited many remote islands in the Caribbean and the Pacific. She likes visiting the Caribbean Islands the best. They are a little warmer and there seems to be a more beautiful tropical foliage. She really likes Palm Trees. Remembering her less than positive Poison Ivy experience. Like the time she landed in an ivy patch one time on the mountains of Oregon. Another bad experience she remembered was of physically ending up in a thorny blackberry patch. She learned from her mistakes and did not want to duplicate them again. Now she sticks to her strict operating procedure of astral projecting and when safe she can teleport. Following this S.O.P. (standard operating procedure) has worked very well for her.

Poppy often returns to a secluded island that is far removed from busy shipping lanes and commercial airline routes. It was the first time she saw a Mermaid lounging on one of the islands. She became friends with them. The Mermaids reside in an ocean area that has not been explored yet. The Mermaids are able to dive and live in the ocean at depths of over 6000 feet. This helps in keeping their existence undetectable and off anyone's radar. It is very dark at those depths. They do however have Bioluminescence and that is what illuminates the outlines of the coral, sponge and creatures. The calm lighting experience is similar to a walk in the moonlight on a warm summer's night along a tiki torch lit path while watching lightning bugs in a field. Diving to these great depths the light is absorbed before it reaches the surface. Mermaids do not feel the cold or pressure when they descend to those depths, because of their scales. Their habitat is close to hot vents at the bottom of the ocean for warmth and use it as an additional energy source. Occasionally mermaids will come to the surface. On one of these trips to the surface a couple mermaids were soaking up the sun and lounging on a beach. With half of themselves in the water mostly their tails. Occasionally splashing their bodies with water, with just a flick of their tails. Poppy could watch them for hours. She is fascinated with the gorgeous sparkly colors of their scales. These scales lay perfectly and flow all the way to their large tails. Systematically flip flopping water onto their bodies. This keeping the mermaids from losing their tails and the transformation from tail to legs if they dry out. This gives them the ability to swim away quickly if disturbed. Normally when Liveling's astral project they are invisible. Some mermaids have the ability to see an aura or ghost like figure. One of the mermaids saw Poppy's Aura. She was not afraid but curious. Poppy felt safe and motioned for them to wait while she teleported so they could carry on a conversation. In her astral form she was unable to talk, she could only gesture. After a long conversation and earning their trust, Poppy was convinced to go with them. The Mermaids have a magic way of taking Poppy into the water and giving her the ability to breathe while under water. She made several trips with them. Poppy does not have the same physiology and cannot withstand the pressure at 6000 feet. They take her to more shallow areas, introducing her to many of their friends and family. She has to Astral Project to see where they actually live. They can see her Aura and are able to communicate telepathically. They also showed her some old undocumented shipwrecks. Many have treasure on them. Mermaids use some of the gems they find on these ships, to make beautiful jewelry, like necklaces and small tiaras designed with beautiful large pearls from Giant Ocean Oysters. All their jewelry is unique and stunning. They also incorporate shells with the gems and pearls. They intertwine them with gold into beautiful ornate pieces of artistic jewelry. Poppy enjoys her many visits with the Mermaids. They show her different shipwrecks and have made her a friendship necklace and tiara. Poppy only wears her tiara when she visits. (See the picture of a necklace above) Obviously it would create too many questions in her village or out in the human world. The pearls are a rare large species not seen.

Poppy liked visiting some of the lakes in Canada. The views with snow covering everything, were breathtaking and there was total isolation. No one around for thousands of miles. She only visited in astral form during the winter months, due to the extreme cold temperatures. On one of these visits she found another clan but only viewed them from afar, for fear of being exposed if she got to close. Some folk tales spoke of this clan. Most of the stories were terrifying and for that reason she wanted to check on them from time to time and only from the viewpoint and cover of the frozen tundra. Not all Liveling type clans are the same. Some have been at war with other clans and have been fighting for centuries. Poppy's clan is very peaceful. They had outgrown fighting centuries ago. There are many stories. One story is of when the Livelings closed themselves off from using the magic doors and quit astral projecting, because these evil clans were going into the Cave of Never Ending Doors and fighting over who would use which doors exclusively. Some of the doors were even created by some warring clans, for that express purpose of spying on and getting the jump on other clans. In the past they were at odds with clans like this. Livelings did not want to be exterminated by another clan, so they had to close themselves off from the doors. For security and preservation. Folk stories were being passed down from generation to generation. These stories are what got Poppy interested. She wanted more information. Finding out about these evil clans, she knew she had to keep checking on them. Especially, to make sure they were not doing anything that would jeopardize any other clan's safety. That was her ultimate goal. She has secluded spots that she goes to, that afforded her camouflage. That way she could observe the clan's undetected, when in her physical form. Other clans she can only check up on them in her astral form. She had to be careful not to be detected, because there are some who can see the auras of others when they are in astral form. She remains vigilant.

There are no grocery or clothing stores at Poppies Liveling home in the mountain valley. All they have is person to person bartering. So when she is traveling to far off places, she needs to blend in while observing humans or other clan's in their home area. The best way is to obtain appropriate clothes so she would not call attention to herself, when in a different demographical area. She uses the special magic doors in the cave to create specific items that will help her to blend in, during her interactions with other clans. The Liveling's are simple beings and their clothes are simple. Made from the material of the surrounding forestation mountain area. They have sheep like creatures for wool clothing, blankets, etc. Obviously not the specific type of costumes Poppy needed. The Liveling clothing is practical but not exciting, all though comfortable. Their wardrobe does not allow her to blend in when she was outside the Liveling area. Poppy enjoys getting costumes for undercover visits to the different areas. It is like "Dress Up" when you were a kid. Some of her costumes include camouflaged apparel that blends into the surroundings, when she is watching small clans and checking on them from afar.

Poppy usually does not need money. When she needed anything she mostly used gold and precious jewels from a cave door-room. Some gems she uses are in its raw unpolished form from her Liveling home and passed down from generation to generation. Poppy's family has gems in great abundance. Some gems and gold are used for decorations in their homes and some for special occasions. Similar to how humans would put fake fruit in a bowl. Some of these gems are the size of plastic apples, pears and grapes normally collecting dust. So her use of the gems went unnoticed. They really have not used gems in decades. They use gems and gold for the occasional wedding or ceremony decorations. Weddings are rare since they live for centuries. Liveling's mate for life and are never separated, except by death. Liveling weddings are always extravagant. They use gems on wedding dresses and Tiaras. For these purposes, they would cut and polish them. In ceremonies, gems are used to provide mostly color. Similar to a floral arrangement. They did not pick flowers since most were friends.

Poppy set up an automatic trust fund. It is the most efficient way to take care of all the bills at her human house. For this she used paper money she created in the currency room. She created this room since paper money and exchange is fairly recent. Gold and gems had worked for what seemed like eons. Using gems would be noticed in the human world and would have caused unwanted attention. Ultimately making it very difficult for her as an outsider. Gems would have made it harder to convert to cash. It would also have meant too many questions that she was not prepared to answer. She had all her bases covered. With all aspects from; the clothes, home and monetary needs. Most importantly using gems would have exposed the Liveling's secret. Money was not needed by the Liveling's. They all live in their symbiotic relationships. A full circle community of taking care of everyone's simple needs from Liveling's to plants and animals.

This is the gem room story. The Gem Room behind this door has jewels of every size and color. Diamonds, rubies, sapphires, emeralds and other gems with beautiful unique colors humans have never even seen. The door itself is beautiful and abstract. Showing almost every precious gem that is inside this oversized room. There is even an artificial light inside the door. This light moves through the gems and creates a color spectrum similar to a rainbow that shines on the wall directly across from the door. These gems in the room are always replenishes the next time she enters the room. Like magic, with the exact amount and sizes she has taken. Even in the same bowl placement in the room. There are large beautifully ornate bowls for each gem. The bowls are made of a magical gold and silver alloy that controls the quality and quantity. Each bowl has specific gems and sizes. There is never a larger ruby with smaller rubies and not even a different type of gem. They are even separated by polished, cut and raw stones. Poppy is set for hundreds of lifetimes. She has a simple and plain wardrobe that does not need loud or attention getting jewelry. She just uses these gems for trading with other clans. Sometimes she will barter for accessories, costumes and essentials to further her façade. Shiny objects were in greater demand for bartering or getting a clan to let their guard down. Poppy showed them how they could use these beautiful colored gems in jewelry or to enhance a simple, plain decoration on an outfit. Some gems are even used for lining paths to accentuate and beautify, you would use river rock. These gems bought her way into the confidence of many clans. One clan had several simple gold bowls. She showed them how they could use the gems to enhance the bowls beauty. Giving them gems made them smile and dance with glee. The Fir Clan and others used these gems for jewelry. Poppy enjoys seeing how each clan has different uses and needs for the gems. She enjoyed her interaction with the Fir and Pine Clans the best. They are the most closely related to the Liveling clan. Even visiting some aunts and uncles who are in the Fir and Pine Clans. They had broken ties many centuries ago. She has really missed her relatives. They were asked to leave because of their notoriously evil ways and to protect the Livelings from the possibility of extinction. Poppy hoped she could reunite these clans and her own someday.

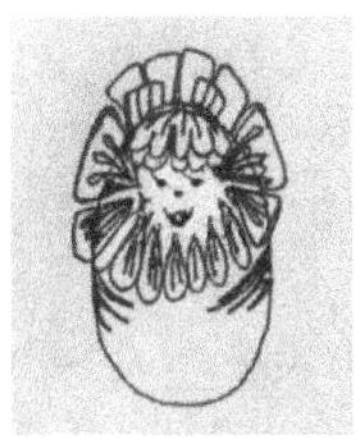

Now lets' get to the best part of Poppy's story, the doors, worlds and the adventures Poppy has. She really likes to go often to the Unusual Item room. It has unique magical type objects. There is a collection of special and unusual objects. There is nothing she would be able to find in a traditional human store. This room has both living and nonliving items on display. Some of the more unique items she enjoys looking at and playing with are in this room. As she browses in this room she spies a potato looking object. The body looks like a smooth shiny potato with a flower face. When she strokes the potato like object on the top of its head, it comes alive. It became her favorite little pet as it makes cute little sighing noises when it moves. It gets little side wrinkles as the body moves from side to side in a swaying motion and does not have any arms or legs. It has a beautiful flower face with enchanting eyes, button nose and a perfectly shaped little mouth. Flower petals surrounding the face give it a whimsical look. Her favorite, has a light pink face, petals with dark purple edges, blue eyes and cute tiny rosy red lips. The face is animated as well. The eyes watch Poppy as she tickles it and it wrinkles its nose and mouth. It has a quiet little laugh along with this warm unique smile. This creature is the sweetest thing/pet and it gives her great joy. When she is done playing with it, she just gives it a tap on the top of the head and it becomes inanimate again. With no movement, it looks like a plastic potato type toy. It does not move when asleep. She could take it anywhere, if not for the Livelings entry and exit rule. It is the perfect portable size for walking around. She can take it out of her pocket, strokes it and enjoys the pure joy of seeing the little face wrinkle and exude pure love. A perfect companion while looking at all the unique items in the room. Only needing to tap it and put it back in her pocket even when picking up another item. No one would ever be the wiser. She is working on a way to remove it from the room. She has not been successful yet.

There is a wide variety of color combinations of these potato type creatures. This one is her favorite creature. This unusual item room has other nonliving/living objects. Some would be easy to fool the normal world. Poppy could just say they are a "piece of art", when not animated. Another little joyful item in this room is the shape and size of a skinny ferret. It looks like a very large caterpillar type creature with emerald green feathers. They are so thick and silky like that of a Cockatoo. It has a pointed snout and when it laughs, it rolls over and she can see its several cute little caterpillar feet type appendages. It has no toes and the feet just come to a soft point. They feel soft like a baby's skin, not slimy. When she tickles its feet and belly, the whole body wriggles and it giggles softly. The colors of all the odd creatures are bright and vibrant. They all look like ceramic or plastic when in sleep mode. It is a joy for her to walk through the room to experience and see all the oddities. Some items are lying down and others are standing upright. The sizes ranges from small and cute to large and ominous. Items are all neatly arranged and organized. There is no room for more. They all seem logically displayed. It looks like everything is artistically placed. Nothing looks out of place or stuffed in to fit. She can see everything without having to peek around, over or under items or from afar. There are even viewing benches to sit on and admire the items. The benches have living floral plants around them that are always fragrant with pretty flowers that always look picture perfect. Poppy can hear the plants and flowers either purr or hum in a very soothing manner. There are never any dead or brown leaves or flowers to distract from the beauty of the surroundings. It is as if they keep regenerating and never die. All the plants and flowers are perfect and don't look like they have ever been picked. Poppy is not sure if they feel pain but did not want to chance it. The flowers are so animated and look alive. She could spend hours in this room and still not see all of the unique creatures or objects. When Poppy does exit the room she has to leave her favorite potato type object. She created a special table next to the door just inside. This makes it easier for her to pick it up first thing after entering the next time.

Another creature that caught Poppy's eye while she was sitting on a bench, was what looks like a small giraffe with long, lanky legs, long neck and similar giraffe coloring. That is where the similarity ended. It actually has three long necks, five legs 2 in front and 3 in the rear and a tail that is like a short peacock's ornate tail. Splashes of colors from red and orange accents at the base of the tail and then it changes to blue and green feathers. These creatures all have whimsical smiles and big teeth, as you would expect to see on a Cheshire-Cat, almost humanlike. They are very animated and can run and jump. The bigger the creature the more agile and movement and capabilities it has. This seemed odd to Poppy. Seeing these large creatures jumping around with their long necks and three heads smiling at her. It was entertaining to watch.

Moving on to the next room. This room has Giant Dragonflies and Butterfly type creatures. Poppy enjoys riding rese creatures. She can choose a fast or slow experience. There are multi colored variations and patterns she has never seen before. The Butterfly creatures are very gentle and move slowly. More of a floating and fluttering of their wings. The

Dragonfly creatures are more hyper in their movement. Two different riding experiences for her in the same room. Butterfly riding is for just killing time and taking in all the beautiful flowers. The Dragonfly ride is for racing and is more exciting. She can cover more ground quickly with a better aerial view over all. These flying creatures are about the size of a small pony. A nice size for someone Poppy's size to ride.

If you love big Lions, you will love this next door and the experience that is a very short distance after walking into this room. Poppy enjoys relaxing next to the small stream with a full sized lion. It is a relaxing atmosphere. She strokes it like you would a domestic cat, while it rests its large head in her lap. They are on a mossy patch of grass next to the clear fresh water stream. There is no fear just total admiration. This is all she does in this world room while stroking the Lion and it purrs in a loving response. She has never explored further.

Another door she explores has creatures, with similarities to a Hippo. Their size is comparable to a large Great Dane, but has pink stripes and an elephant type nose. When its nose explores Poppy's legs, it is soft and gentle as though it was caressing a baby, but it did leave a little nose slime. However, she does enjoy the experience. It is just as cute and cuddly as the next creature. It loves to be in the water and on land equally. No mud in this world. So a very clean experience when riding it. Poppy enjoys many doors/room/worlds, where she gets to ride some type of creature.

There is a creepy section of this room that she stays away from. Poppy saw it was way back behind another open doorway. She could not see inside this room past the doorway. There is a fog barrier. One day she took the plunge and did venture inside. The door did not detract from the peaceful and tranquil atmosphere of the magical room surroundings. When this door caught her eye again she walked into it. The immediate feeling was not tranquil and far from peaceful. It was not really evil, but close. Evil is what you make of it and even cute and cuddly can be used for evil in the wrong hands. Her one and only experience was of when she saw an Alligator type creature. As it flew closer with large black feathered wings it was scary and it had big sharp needle like teeth. This long mouth like an alligator was snapping at her. As if that was not bad enough, it had long talons extending out from its toes and red eyes that looked demonic. That is the only creature Poppy saw before she exited quickly. That was the one and only time she was curious and went into that opening. There are tales of Liveling's going into that room and never coming out again. Bad things are reported to have happened in that room. So terrible they don't even speak of it. Just bits and pieces of info told in the fire pit stories.

Now back to Poppy's rural human house. Her house looks like any other house on a private woodsy block. It has a very plain exterior and there is nothing that drew attention to it. It blends into the rest of the block. Hidden by trees and hedges. No one can even see the house when driving or walking by the yard. There is a mossy type grass that does not grow much and does not need to be cut. The plants create a privacy hedge that is about ten foot tall. All greenery in the yard was easy care so no need for upkeep or maintenance. If you were able to see the house it would appear to look like a one story, 1200 square foot ranch style house. To tell Poppy's story is to tell you about her house and the many doors with rooms attached to them. Poppy has a secret way into the house through one of the magic doors or she teleports. Her house security starts with the foyer and a massive, uniquely chiseled marble table that is perfectly placed in her foyer with no chairs. The only function of this table is for strategic security and not dining. Poppy had to create and teleport the table into the foyer. She created this oversized table to fit perfectly and to the exact specifications of the room. The move was very tricky since she did not allow any space for herself. She did however want it to be wedged in tight. She had to create a space under the table so she could strategically teleport it into an eight by eight square room. She than created an ornate crystal chandelier to go above the table. It looks similar to very thin antlers with many sharp spikes. It is also enormous and created in a square shape to engulf the entire remaining space over the table. All this was for only one purpose and that is her security. No one could push their way in like salesmen or nosey neighbors. There is no room to even open the doors at either end.

To complete her security measures she has intercom access panels by each door inside her house and by each of the Never Ending Cave doors. With this system she has the ability to oversee the interior, exterior and the Never-Ending Cave of Doors. Poppy always speaks to visitors from intercoms that have a one way video system.

When she does leave her house occasionally, it is by a secretly hidden and invisible door. This door is located on the side of the house. She never leaves by the front door. Usually she teleports. This is the most secure means.

Just past the secured foyer and her massive kitchen there is a visual into an expanse that is unbelievable. Large cathedral ceilings and expansive rooms, like a huge castle.

Past Poppy's kitchen is a hallway. This unbelievably long hallway gives the appearance of looking into a mirror and gives the illusion of an image that goes on forever. This is Liveling magic. There is an entire world within a small space, with a life time of exploration and wonders. To really tell this story I need to take you from door to door and door to room. Each room is more bizarre and spectacular than the previous. Poppy has favorite rooms and visits them quite often. There are particular rooms that she does not venture into as much. Other door-rooms are whole complete worlds. (More on this later)

The room behind the blocked entry is Poppy's enormous kitchen. With a 30 foot high ceiling and 150 foot wide. It is huge and gives some perspective of the massive

expanse that is inside this tiny house facade. When she enters
her large kitchen she can see it has all the gadgets, accessories
and necessities. Some she has never seen or used. Many are
still in cupboards and cabinets. The kitchen has self-cleaning
dinner ware, pots, silverware, etc. When Poppy is done
cooking or eating she just holds up the utensil, plate or pot and
let's go of it. It rises to the ceiling and after she leaves the
room it mysteriously cleans and puts itself away. That makes
for a very clean and never messy kitchen. This is an amazing
house with so many fantastic magical rooms. She really does
not spend much time cooking but does enjoy the occasional
bowl of ice cream with fudge topping. A delicacy Livelings do
not have access to.

The room off the kitchen is very large with a huge
walk-in fireplace and an equally large stone mantle to match.
This mantle is about 10 foot high. The oversized shelves are
neatly filled with large whimsical and ornamental art work.
The smaller vases, and artifacts are on lower smaller shelves.
The larger artifacts are up higher. So she can see them better
from below. Many of these items and art pieces have been in
her family for eons. They hold a lot of sentimental value for
her as well. Many are one of a kind relics. Her parents never
talked about them and she cannot ask anything about them or
her secret would be out. To see items up close on the mantle or
other shelves she just needs to step on to the wooden stool next
to the fireplace. It lifts her up to enable a closer look. The stool
is very steady so no chance of falling. It has a thin wooden
ornately carved handle. She holds onto the handle when she
wants to lean a little closer for a better look at the amazing
craftsmanship of an item or if she wants to move something.
The carvings in the stone fireplace are smooth, due to centuries
of use. The stone mantle looks Viking in origin, with carvings
of ancient ships, horns and real jewel incrusted armor plating
that is made of gold.

Beyond this room is a Living room with a massive,
natural deep rock pool and a small rock island in the center.

The island looks like an iceberg with more rock below the surface and crystal clear water. Oversized couches surround one side. This rock pool is stream fed. It comes from a small hole in the wall. She is not sure where it originates, but the natural water pool motif living room is awesome. It is like having her own private mini lake.

Poppy never has to clean the cave or house beyond the foyer. The foyer is blocked from the magic to clean. In fact the more dust the better. It adds to the look of abandoned house, so less visitors. This is the only place you will see dust. Dust only visible through tiny narrow, vertical windows that are visible from the outside of the house. There is no dust on any of the relics on the mantle or anywhere else. This is due to the fireplace is a flying feather duster. One of many. They are activated by any kind of dust. Anytime a little dust particle appears a duster will fly up and devour it. That is better than spreading the dust around, like you would with a normal feather duster. Throughout the house and cave hallways there are some beautifully colored feather dusters. All shapes, sizes and personalities with unique color combinations. Under the pretty feathers, ribbons and ornately carved wooden handles are beautiful mouths, that enjoy eating dust. They live only to eat dust, which makes for a really clean residence. Poppy has seen them dancing and flying about at all hours of the day and night. Catching those nasty dust mites and dust bunnies or whatever dust animals may be lurking about. The dusters are very stealth and make no noise at all while going about their business of only eating dust. There is something very ethereal about the way they move and float about. Never fast or frantic. More like they are dancing to music. Poppy never heard anything. It was fascinating and inspiring when she observes several dusters meeting up to clean. She noticed they dip and sway in sync as if to the beat of the same musical tune.

Now it is time to explore the magical doors that are attached to the house by special Liveling magic. This magic connects the Liveling clan to the cave doors and Poppy's home in the human world. Some rooms beyond these doors have entire worlds behind them. Others are very small and cozy rooms. It would take a lifetime to explain all of them. Only Livelings can enter or exit these doors. Once inside the larger worlds the doorway will close when a Liveling walks in about twenty feet or so. The door itself will disappear. It will always reappear when they get back within 20 feet of the opening. This way the door does not detract from the surroundings. It does not work that way for the items, creatures, etc. inside. It is impossible for them to leave any room. The twenty foot rule will only activate in the presence of a Liveling and only a Liveling can exit. It is something in there genetic makeup. In addition the genetics of the creatures and items cannot exit or summon the exit doors. If a door is opened by a Liveling, there appears to be an invisible force field. It prevents items or creatures from exiting. Poppy has heard stories of lost Livelings that ventured to far from the exit point and got lost. They will be lost in that world forever, unless they can return to within 20 foot of the exit. Only then will the door reappear and allows them to leave. That is another reason it is forbidden to explore the magical doors. More information later on Poppy's markings of the exits to assure an exit door will reappear.

Another very odd door leads to a world with a very small Island surrounded by an ocean that extends as far as the eye can see. This island is full of tiny crab type creatures that are a combination of human and crab. Having crab type legs. One small pincher and the other arm with a huge claw that is

1/2 the size of their body. A large human face and not proportionate at all. They move like crabs as they scurry across the ground. Others stand on their two rear legs to get what looked like berries from a tree. When Poppy approached they all scurried under the tree cover for protection. She could see the creatures and they are approximately 6 inches wide. On this island there was a forest of Ponytail Palm type trees. The majority of the trees are only four to five foot tall. An appropriate size with the crab creatures. The trees have an umbrella type canopy with smooth red bark. This kept the ground area shaded. The island itself is only 50 foot wide X 100 foot long and completely surrounded by water. The door lead to the center of the island. Poppy followed a path that leads to one end of the island and to the water's edge. There were very small shallow ponds formed in larger flat rocks. The ponds are less than an inch deep. Small waterfalls are cascading from the top tier pool to the others. These pools are approximately four inches to one foot in diameter and ¼ to 1 inch deep. It looked like they are fed by a stream coming from within the forest. Poppy cannot confirm this since she cannot fit under the trees or see through the heavy canopy cover.

The interior of this island has small raccoon type creatures with a cute friendly face. Normal sized birds who are giant in comparison to the crab creatures. Poppy did see the birds carry off a couple. Occasionally it would rain in this tiny world and that is how Poppy believes the tiny streams are created. There is an odd phenomenon. When it rains, small and large bubbles would form on the top of the surrounding ocean water. Not sure why but all the animals ran from these bubbles. Maybe something from below was creating this. She did not stay long enough to find out. As she was leaving she saw the backside of the island and it had tall cliffs with caves. Similar to the ancient Indians living in the cliffs of Utah and Arizona only on a much smaller scale. Poppy had to bend down to get really close to see into the cave dwellings. These caves were filled with hundreds of crab creatures. She left quickly and did not return to this creepy door again.

The Spider Door is one she spent very little time in as well. She does not like Arachnids. Some of the spiders behind this door were the size of cars. So as soon as she saw hundreds of spiders that size, she immediately exited and she never returned again. Marking it with a red face☺. More on these magic markings which will be explained later.

Poppy heard other tales of exploring Liveling's, who not only picked the wrong door but they picked them for evil reasons. One such door is of an upside down world that as soon as a Liveling entered, they are thrown to the sky. Large evil creatures are flying around waiting to devour all the magic energy from eating a Liveling. With nothing to catch the Liveling and if they did not react quickly enough or adjust their equilibrium, they would never return to tell their story or be heard from again. They were led to this world and to their deaths by warring clans who miss represented what experience this world would provide. No one really knows for sure what transpired. Stories were always be made up and added onto. The tales over years evolve and grow in intensity, to make for a scarier story.

Other doors have monsters of various types and sizes. When a Livelings organs are either partially or fully eaten or decapitated, it is a very gruesome demise tale. This is the only way for a Liveling to die. There are many early exploration stories they tell around the fire pit at night, to scare the Younglings. Poppy is not sure if they told these stories to entertain or scare, but it did both. Yet, Poppy still wanted more. It made her very curious but cautious. She is compelled to explore further. She does not want the same fate as some of her ancestors. She proceeds cautiously by not venturing too far in past the doors especially the ones that have whole worlds. She is also very careful to leave a marker that she can see from several hundred feet or even miles away. Being afraid someone or something will move or remove it. Poppy decided to create a sturdier marker. Especially since the last one had problems with blowing over in the wind. If she wants to go further in to a world, it is necessary to make a stationary more permanent marker, out of harder wood or light weight metal. This is easy for her to create. All she has to do is visualize the marker and it appears or she can tweak and update the markers occasionally as needed, when and if circumstances changed. It is always a work in progress. She must be able to see the markers during the day. It must be a luminescent beacon she can see it after darkness falls. Some of the worlds have a very short day to night cycle. Very different from the human world. There can be several sunrise and setting cycles. It makes for multiple and beautiful experience of sunsets and sunrises in a short period of time. It is very important that a colorful cloth is sometimes used to attach the marker to a tree or structure that make it extra sturdy. So far it has been working for her. Poppy still remains cautious and never strays far. She never enters the doors she has marked dangerous or evil. This way Poppy knows which doors she should and should not enter, by listening to the many stories she has heard while growing up. Poppy pieced together information on specific styles of doors to stay away from and only returns to the doors she is familiar with and knows are safe. But after hundreds of visits to the same doors, she is starting to get very bored and needs new adventures. Especially since she has unlimited access to the doors. More information on this when I tell you about her friend Iris.

Another world Poppy visits has a waiting room that you walk into and stand while waiting to board a mini train. A small version they have at theme parks. It chugs slowly through a beautiful countryside filled with stars in the moon lit sky. It is a theme park atmosphere and in the distance she can see approximately five castles perched on top of tall narrow pinnacles that look like fingers of a hand. The train chugs to the top slowly and laboriously. When she reaches the first castle the train pulls into a small station with a Knights of the Round Table theme. When she walks into the castle it is filled with music and looks like a Renaissance Fair. There is dancing in the center and long tables filled with large amounts of food, gold, silver and gem incrusted goblets and plates. All are wearing appropriate costumes for this theme. A large fitting room is in a side room for her to pick out whatever she wishes. From jousters to queen outfits are all available. What costume she picks effects the outcome of what experience Poppy will have. There is an accessory room with flower headdresses and long ribbons to swords and armor. There is a small jousting ring with tiny ponies and lances made of a very soft rubber type substance that looks similar to a large round candy sucker on a stick.

The second castle is made of scrumptious edible candy and has bright colors. The entrance has huge double front doors, made of shiny pulled sugar with heavy hinges, resembling the ribbon sugar candy at Christmas. These are huge multi colored festive candy bows. Long flowing ribbon railings, furniture and art pieces. Some red and orange candy fire torches, lighting that gives the appearance of flickering fires, throughout this candy castle. Chandeliers made of sugar strips that look like colorful crystal pieces, hanging from the ceiling. When Poppy eats something, it magically regenerates. In the center of the castle are small rides. A tiny train, twirling tea cups and miniature merry-go-round with whimsical animals in all the colors of a rainbow. The ribbon candy floors are very colorful with stripes of different combinations in each room.

The third castle looks like giant ice cream cones. Similar to the Moscow building in Russia without the points on top. The surrounding temperature is pleasant as all the other castles are. When she eats any ice cream it is magically regenerated. Poppy can see giant bowls of colored sprinkles and toppings for the hard and soft ice cream that is available.

The fourth castle has a rustic cabin look and feel. Small forest animal type creatures are running around free and loose, similar to a petting zoo with no restraints or pens. All the animals are colorful. Some even have purple spots. Hot chocolate available along with candy corn.

The fifth castle has more of an island feel. Ponds, palm trees and bright colored birds flying around inside very high ceilings of glass that make it look like the sun is always shining with a comfortable warm atmosphere. A giant Avery filled with many different types of birds, flying and perched on tree limbs.

Behind another door she visited regularly, is a green rolling hill setting, with creatures similar to deer, in varying shades of purple with shorter legs, so they are more evenly matched when running alongside of Poppy. They have long flowing hair that shimmers and flows beautifully, like a horse's long mane, floating when running or standing dramatically on a mountain top on a windy day. Their face and head is puppy like. So of course she would find them cute and endearing. These creatures can run, jump, roll in the grass and play with her when she wants a little more physical interaction, rather like you would play with puppies. It is a larger world. Poppy has not had time to explore all of it yet and she did not want to get lost. Always being careful to look back over her shoulder to see the marker that she set up. There are no trees to attach a marker to. That made her a little leery of going in to far. Poppy created a tree for the sole purpose of attaching a marker to it. Plus being the only tree in this world, made it even more visible at 100 feet high. She does enjoy running and playing with these creatures. She gets a lot of frustrations out this way. They are so cute and she has fun with them. She always felt great after she left this room. Always with a more positive feeling. It seems like the creatures always knew when she had enough. They would just bound off over the hills and disappear. She never really knew where they went. All she knew is when she enters through the door, the creatures are there and ready to play. That is enough for her for now.

One of the cozy comfortable rooms that Poppy visits quite often is the Fluffy Pet room. Inside are pink, purple and blue colored, fuzzy, fluffy ball creatures covered with soft fur similar to a mink or fox. They make soft purring like sounds and have no features like arms or legs, so they do not jump. They bounce around until she picks them up and puts them on her lap. They love to be cuddled and petted. Since they cannot jump. Poppy picks up which ones she wants to relax with on the couch. The room always smells like baby powder and has several large lounges made with tuck and roll, in a half circle design, approximately eight foot across. These lounges are to recline on while enjoying the company of the fuzzy ball creatures. She goes there when she needs to unwind and relax. There are a few that she favors and they are the larger ones. This is a relaxed setting that is less physical than some of the other rooms. Poppy just lays back on a lounge and lets the cute fuzzy balls bounce and wiggle all around her. They do not weigh much. The biggest ones weigh approximately twelve ounces. Most of them are about the size of a small honey dew melon. The smallest one weighs about 1 ounce and is the size of a walnut. Poppy enjoys the larger ones they give her a more penetrating massage than the smaller ones. Poppy is in control of which ones are allowed on the lounge. She just loves to watch them as they bounce all her cares away, while making a soft purring type noise. One time she spent about two hours with them. She had a lot to sort out on that day. The larger balls of fluff managed to bounce and coo her frustrations away. The lighting is soft so she is unable to see very far past the lounges. The lighting is very subtle, like you would expect in a spa setting. She always made time for this room.

The Dragon room has a loveable, wise, magical dragon named Sordo. His room is easy to find because of the large dragon carved into the golden door, with large precious, bright green emeralds for his friendly eyes. Poppy goes to him when she needs advice or a friendly ear. He will just listen when she just needs to talk. He is someone to have an intelligent conversation with. He is very old, wise and knows a lot about the history of the Cave of Never Ending Doors. Poppy asked him once, how old he was. He said "As old as time", and would not explain further. Someday she will ask for more on his age. The dragon meetings are in a cave like setting. It has a high rounded rock ceiling. The cave is tubular with a flat floor in areas which make it easier for Poppy to walk on and to carry on these conversations. She does not know how far back the cave goes or even if it has an exit. Poppy has never asked him that, because he is always reluctant to answer personal questions. She only knows that when she needs the dragon and opens the door he is always there and always eager to help or console. He commands a proud crown of golden metallic looking feathers that have the appearance of an actual crown of gold. He has a whimsical soft face. Sordo never looks angry or upset. His voice is soft, pleasant, calming and never harsh. He is more like a teacher. That she can talk to him about anything and he gives her suggestions on any subject she is inquisitive or concerned about. Poppy always leaves his cave feeling so much better than she did when she came in. Sordo also helps her pick which doors to explore and which doors to stay away from (in addition to all the stories she has heard growing up). Of course along with Sordo's affirmations and expertise. He has told her horrible stories about grotesque and evil beings that lurk behind some of the doors. She takes his advice and does not enter those doors. She has also tried to mark all the doors she has been to or heard about with a warning to herself and others that may come after her. Some stories are far too gruesome and will not be include in this account. Whenever Sordo sees that Poppy's demeanor changes, when they were talking, he would switch to a more positive story. He just wanted to inform her so she would not make a bad decision or enter an evil door. He would not dwell on the negative. It physically made her shiver to even think about it. That is the time when Poppy needed two hours to relax in the Fluffy Pet Room. Poppy's marks explain what is behind each of the doors. These marks have a simple meaning behind each one. They are magically invisible to anyone who is not a Liveling. The marks only react to the presence of magical beings. Of course that means the good with the bad can see the marks. Poppy and Sordo came up with simple ones. If someone was running down the hall of doors, the marks would not be visible. When standing still in front of a door or walking slowly by, the mark would be visible. Letting Liveling's know whether the door was evil and dangerous or good. Of course there is free will. There is a choice, but they have to deal with the consequences. Back to the meanings and what the marks look like. A simple green ☺ Smiling face for good doors. A blue face ☹ for those unfriendly doors. A Red face ☺ if it is bad and a Black X for danger. Poppy updates a few door marks once in a while to further explain the world behind the door. By adding or updating these marks, she will know what her experiences were or will be. Poppy really enjoyed being able to add a green ☺ Smiling face marker to a door. That meant more doors she could return to.

After decades of visiting Sordo the dragon, Poppy had never seen another dragon. On one visit she saw something sparkly and it distracted her attention. Suddenly there was about half dozen smaller dragons, about the size of a large dog. These colorful dragons were peaking at her from behind a boulder. They suddenly they caught Poppy's eye when they all flew out in a flash of color. Each had a beautiful color of skin and scales that sparkled as if they were covered with little diamonds or precious stones. The smaller dragons color are similar to green emeralds, blue sapphires, red rubies, yellow topaz, pink diamonds and not to forget the purple amethyst color. The cave just exploded in color. When they started flying in a graceful swirling movement as if to music, Poppy questioned Sordo. Who are they? Finally with a pause he imparted to her, they are his children. She mentioned, they are so beautiful. He looked very proud. They had kept behind the rocks and were not visible before. After sizing Poppy up and feeling comfortable with her, they became curious. They landed and wanted to meet her. They came close and sniffed her, to get her scent. Dragons can sense a person's emotional state with a scent and can even sense that person telepathically from miles away. From now on the young dragons were present during Poppy's visits with Sordo. It is always visually pleasing and relaxing for her to watch them flying around the cave. The young dragons dart around coming very close to the smooth gray rock with precise precision. Coming within inches of the sides of the cave. Quite the aerial production and show. They never really display any interest in her talks with Sordo. After that first encounter she just enjoys watching them while talking with Sordo. They are never distracting only soothing. Poppy gave them nicknames that are similar to their colors (Emerald, Sapphire, Ruby, Topaz, Pinks and Amy) Amethyst looks like an Amy. She is the shyest one. Sordo never gave Poppy their names, because their names are unpronounceable unless you are a dragon. The smaller young dragons seemed to be fine with the nick names Poppy gave them. They would even do an extra swoop when their name was mentioned. It seemed like they were playing a game of swoop when their name is called. This gave Poppy great joy.

The winter lodge door has a picturesque private lake surrounded by a huge forest with sparkly white snow on the trees and ground. It looks like a winter wonderland that is right out of a painting. In the main lobby area are several oversized picture windows that are 30 foot wide and 20 foot high. A wall of windows looking out at the majestic winter scene. The cathedral ceilings are very high, with large wooden support beams, similar to those you would see at a ski lodge. It is a lighter wood more like white oak that has been smoothed and polished. No rough edges or snags. It is a very relaxed, pleasant atmosphere. There are life size animal carvings, sculptured from wood. These statues are of wilderness scenes throughout the lodge. Next to the big picture window there are five wooden carved trees, varying in size from five to eight foot tall and on both sides of the window. Smaller carvings of woodsy creatures that are real life sized of animals that look similar to wolves, mountain lions and deer. Other rooms may have smaller animals like rabbits and birds. The detail is amazing, down to the creature hairs, feathers and whiskers.

There is a small waterfall running into a stream with rocks that are covered with moss. The stream runs to the other side of the picture window and behind the trees. The room is dimly lit, with what appears to be stars in the ceiling, giving the appearance of an endless sky and a rising moon. It provides more than enough lighting. Poppy can walk down the very wide hall and see the oversized pieces of furniture. All hand carved Opal Oak, with beautiful intricate patterns. All the furniture has overstuffed cushions made with such colorful fabric. No dull browns and beige but have bright abstract patterns and colors. The hallway leads to a natural hot springs that feeds into a spa type pond, with an outdoor motif of big round rocks and small gentle waterfalls cascading down into small inviting pools. Smooth flat rocks close to the edge for lounging on. Surrounding the water ponds are real plants. This gives the appearance of being outside, especially with the open starry sky realistic look in the ceiling that is throughout the lodge, even in the bathrooms. The water temperature is always just right. Never to hot or too cold. Just like lounging in a warm bath. It melts Poppy's cares away. The water is always the perfect temperature for her. Just around the corner are the towels. They are in a private hidden mirrored area, for dressing and undressing. A very cozy area with rounded sides and cathedral ceiling. It felt like being in an underground cave but it was not claustrophobic at all, room for large crowds but she had it all to herself. The pool area is dimly lit everywhere but this mirrored area. The lights only get brighter when she approaches and needs the additional lighting. It gave the appearance of a moonlight atmosphere, while relaxing and enjoying the pools. The floor is a natural slate throughout the lodge. Natural warm springs run under the slate and that is how the floors stayed warm.

The bedroom suites are each more unique and luxurious than the next. Having very large furniture with ornately carved headboards and night stands. In addition to the furniture are wild animal scenes, in the corner of every suite. The animal scenes are carved out of wood and a stone type quartz. Such great attention to detail. These sculptures are on a smaller scale. The smaller animals are carved to represent fox and rabbits and are life size as well, that are arranged in a nature scene, far in the corner. Intermixed with real plants and flowers. The rooms are huge and about four times the size of a normal bedroom suite. They never feel tight for space, even with all the sculptures and oversized furniture. The suites also have warm slate floors and rugs in many colors. Some rugs have the thickness of four to five inches and are soft, like a fox fur, but is artificially created and no animals were harmed. It is always a pleasurable experience for Poppy to feel the soft sensation between her toes. She tries to spend the night in a different room each stay. The multiple suites are always changing. She does not have to go that far in to the lodge for change. Poppy always felt very secure in the fact she would not get lost. Since the lodge type setting has boundaries and with the information she gets from Sordo, the dragon, gives her the freedom to explore the lodge more freely.

The Disco Room has a simple disco ball hanging from the ceiling over a wooden dance floor, with bright lights and loud disco music. Sometimes when Poppy has nervous energy, she just makes a quick visit for a few disco moves, laughs and leaves feeling energized.

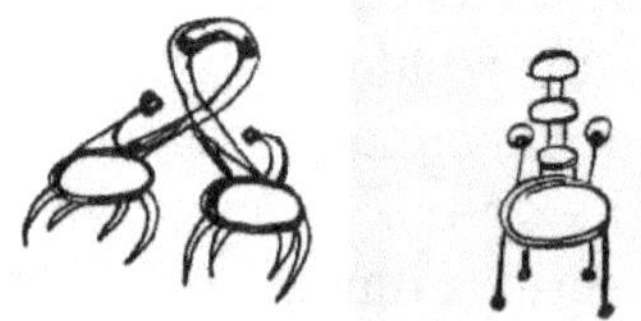

Behind the Musical Chair door is a room that is fun. Poppy wishes she could go more often, but only seems to visit it occasionally. It is filled with whimsical contemporary style chairs in vibrant metallic colors of gold and silver with green, crimson and midnight blue accents. The cushions are a well-groomed suede type fabric, with accent colors that perfectly enhance the metal chair colors. The chairs are always well groomed and polite. No chips or scratches in their paint. No dingy fabric. It is always a pleasure to attend this positive up beat musical room. The chairs dance about the room to music, bending and swaying to the rhythm. Poppy can see at a glance, they all have different personalities. She has enjoyed getting to know each chair personally. The double chair sides even have two separate personalities. Being in this room always leaves her very upbeat and exhilarated. If the music is fast and furious, Poppy would sometimes dance with the chairs. If asked, she would sit on them and go for a whirling ride. Some chairs just swayed to the music. All of the chairs were unique in their design and it matched their personalities. The music is always uplifting. The double chairs that are attached and (pictured above) are very odd but hilarious to watch as they/it moves across the floor and into the air. When the sitting part of the chairs move together and then apart, to the beat of the music it looks similar to a caterpillar. It moves its legs in a bending and swaying motion. The double chair quickly swirls around in what looks like a choreographed and rehearsed dance move. It is a very exhilarating and exciting experience. She never sees an orchestra or band. The music seems to just come out of the walls, ceiling and floor. She can feel the beat of the music. It is never too loud. The magical tunes just cloaked her in a fury of excitement. Poppy tries to join in, as often as she can. The chair seen above to the right, just bounces up and down. Like a teapot letting off steam. She never sits on that chair, but it makes her laugh.

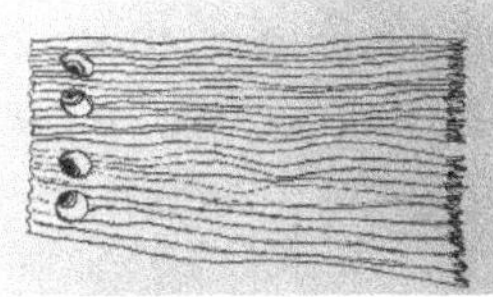

The Rug Creature door is a long narrow room about 30 foot long and 12 foot wide. There are two creatures. Each one is five foot wide and have subtle differences. They are low to the floor and side by side. Each has long flowing hair type locks that are as long as the room and take up most of the floor area. There is a narrow walking area on one side only. This lane is about two foot wide. Poppy has to be very careful not to step on them. In fact she has to turn sideways occasionally, so she did not accidently step on the creature closest to her. Their rippling movement of their long hair often went into the two foot walking area. Their rippling on the floor does not look like a moving carpet. It is more like looking at a watery stream with a creepy twist. They are dark green with a maroon bottom edge, two gentle but goofy and oversized round cartoonish eyes at the top of one end. Poppy is not sure what they actually do or their purpose. Sometimes she will just go to this room and look at them to see if they are doing anything different. When she enters the room, the two large eyes always just follow her as she walks along the side of the room. She thought it was very creepy and never sees them doing anything different. So she will keep checking, because she is curious and feels that someday she will catch them doing something different, though she is not sure what. They are aloof but give her their full, undivided attention. All four eyes always intently follow her. She is not sure if they have a purpose. They must have an underlying reason. Right?

Poppy does not need a garbage service for her human house. She has a garbage room. That's right, a garbage eating room. She does not even need to open the main door for the smaller items. She just opens the drop down hatch and it is gone. If she has something larger. She opens the large metal door with heavy duty hinges. After she lays the garbage on the floor, it just disappears. She cannot see the back of the room. It looks like it goes on forever, like a black hole. All she knows is that every time she opens the door with more garbage the previous garbage that she left before is gone. No trace, not even a crumb. The room is spotless. The sides and floor look like it is made of some kind of black metal. It has a very shiny and sterile appearance. Poppy often stops to ponder after she closes the door and starts to leave. She wonders what kind of being or monster eats the garbage. Even when she immediately opens the door and obviously whatever she left before, is gone. It is, like magic. When her mind wonders to scary creepy monsters, she stops herself and moves on before she freaks out to much. She just knows the garbage is gone. Or is it?

Livelings enjoy a few human luxuries, like lamps, tables, chairs and mattresses, but with a magical moss type stuffing. Most of these items have a magical twist. Obviously they were from a door-room in the magical cave from the past. It was so long ago. That the truth became a fire pit story after eons. So no one really knows for sure how or when the furniture was obtained. They usually did not ask the question and it never came up in conversation. Strange that all their furniture lasts for eons. It is magic furniture.

While Poppy is exploring the doors she also leads her dual life with the Livelings. This is very difficult for her, leading two different lives. If she stays away from her family and friends for very long she is missed. So she must go thru the motions of her life with family, friends, human house and doors. She still explores whenever she gets the chance.

Her people the Livelings live a relatively simple life. They coexist with nature, animals and magical creatures, like the Forest Fairies. Livelings don't have houses, but simple dwellings that blend into the countryside, so they will not be detected. Most Liveling homes have been passed down for generations. Some live in carved out cave dwellings or underground caves. This is not enough stimuli to keep Poppy's creative imagination flowing strong. She needs to feed her it, with her access to the human world and witnessing modernization when she astral projected. This allows her imagination to grow and evolve. Her ancestors had updated their lives many years before with some simple luxuries they still use. Most Livelings live in the here and now of the forest and have lost the will to astral project anymore. They all enjoy their simple lives. Where they get the human influence, is in their home furnishings with a twist. They do enjoy the creature comforts of a bed with a mattress, chest of drawers and lamps. No need to have any clocks or appliances. They tell time with a sundial type apparatus which has been used for centuries and it is more accurate. They also have other furniture, like chairs, couches and tables. Couches and mattresses have a unique moss type filling and the fabric coverings are a wool type woven linen blend. They magically stay clean and perfect. Never a need to replace mattresses or pillows. The colors are dull and blend in with the forest surroundings. Too boring for Poppy. That is why she is obsessed with exploring and the visual stimuli of all the colors she has had the pleasure of experiencing.

They do not have any computer type items. There is no need to keep in touch with e-mails. They are not real concerned about time or schedules because they are simple folk and have a sense of when family or community meetings are. It is like they have an internal clock and are never late for anything. Telepathy plays a big part in this sense.

Appliances are another thing that would be impossible to use, since they have no need for electricity. They do have a phosphorous or bioluminescent material that works in the lamps instead of a light bulb. Only activating and lighting up when it gets dark. The light provided is soft and never to bright. More like a lightning bug glow. They don't even need to cover the lamps because they also double for night lights.

When washing clothes, they have a special magic washing pond. A stream runs through the pond. This is also how the pond water stays clean. They do not use any insecticides or poisons. Nothing toxic that would hurt the environment, only natural cleansers. Their clothes dry almost instantly in the sun. Livelings enjoy this quiet time communing with nature and with some of the forest animals who observed them from the shore line.

Their mode of transportation is in the trees. They have rope and twig configured chairs with an elaborate pulley system that is in some of the tallest trees. This takes them to the gardens quite quickly. The pulley system they use is very simple but effective in taking them to where most of the food and vegetables are grown. Livelings are vegetarians. The rest of the day to day schedule is pretty simple. They live in harmony with nature and the animals. In fact they are able to telepathically communicate with all of the animals and do not really need to talk. Livelings are very sensitive and know what animals and each other are thinking or feeling. The animals know they have nothing to fear from them. If an animal is hurt they usually come to Livelings for help. They do have a specific Liveling that is very good at healing the sick and injured animals. Poppy's mother, Daisy, is the healer. She is the one who set up the special healing area. Telepathically they all know where this area is, like an invisible beacon.

The Liveling's themselves do not really get sick. There is the occasional scrape or broken bone, but not much past that. They all are very healthy. It is in their DNA, which translates into longevity. Daisy is a few centuries old, as well as Snap Dragon, Poppy's father. The Liveling clan are not in great number. Large numbers of Liveling's would be harder to keep secret. Also evil clans would seek them out and exterminate them. They are very telepathic and that is mostly how they communicate. Talking is almost unnecessary. They do consider it rude to invade another's private thoughts unless welcomed to do so. That is how Poppy keeps her secret life from her parents and others. She can block them from reading her mind and thoughts.

Enough about family for now. On to the Hot Springs door and what is behind it. Immediately after entering this door she sees a hot springs, with small pools of warm water. Surrounded by round smooth rocks. It is fun to go there when she doesn't mind some company. There is a family of monkey like creatures that live in this world. I say monkey like, because they have bright red bodies with purple accents around there face, nose and mouth. They physically resemble monkeys and have piercing green eyes that are full of mischief, especially the smaller youngster. Their fur is so soft, bright red and they look like little fires darting about. Their front arms are longer than our human world monkeys. So they can wrap their arms around Poppy easily from further away to pull her in. They are very friendly primate creatures and don't mind sharing their hot springs. They clearly are very curious and they will come over and touch different parts of Poppy's body that are different from theirs. Like ears, noses and arms, all while making a sound that is best described as a giggle. The air is warm with a calm breeze, so she does not get cold. The wind dries her hair and body off quickly so there is no need for a towel. It is a nice feeling and never uncomfortable. Poppy never even shivers. The monkey creatures are happy about this phenomenon as well. The water is full of rare minerals that leave their hair and skin feeling soft. Poppy also observes pale blue fish with green stripes and bright yellow accent spots, swimming in the water. They .remind her of Koi. They never seem to bother her or the monkey type creatures. It is very calming to watch them.

Since Poppy cannot see much in the distance due to the steam rising from the warm water, she had never ventured further than the warm springs in all the times she had visited. Finally she decided to see what was beyond the vast steam clouds of the springs. Looking back constantly to make sure she would not lose sight of the rising steam. She, would use the steam as a marker to find her way back, so she would not get lost. Poppy had to travel for better than two hours to get past the steam. Finally the terrain started to change. At first it was very subtle changes that were detectable. Then it was like night and day, as if there were a line drawn between terrains. The colors, temperature and even the smell in the air was foreboding. She kept walking in a straight line and could still see the steam for miles behind her. Suddenly it all changed abruptly. Barely any distance between each side. With high mountain peaks, snowy tops on one side and deep crevices on the other side. It seemed like there was no bottom, as she walked along a narrow path between the two sides. She heard hissing sounds coming from the deep crevices. There was an offensive smell that was so vile. The colors of both sides were strangely dark with bright accents. One side of red, orange and gold. The other side had blue and green with silver streaks. The temperature was very hot. It was extremely hard for her to breathe, as if the air was thinner. One side had peaks that went straight up. The other side had what looked like white snow. Or was it? Finding that hard to believe because of the temperatures, Poppy was afraid to continue. It was not an inviting feeling but one of danger. The feeling she was getting from the surroundings was of imminent danger. Poppy quickly turned around and at a quickened pace went back to the calm surroundings of the warm springs and the cute little monkey creatures. Poppy slid into the water and was embraced by the monkey like creatures. Immediately she became calm in the monkey creatures embrace. They could sense her tension. One of them held her as a caring mother would. She sat there for quite a while. After they gave her comfort from this experience and she felt calmer, she exited the room. In fact, she never visited that door again. She just could not get the feeling out of her mind and every time she passed that door, the memory of the smells and bad feelings came rushing back. Poppy decided there were other more positive doors she would rather explore. Doors that made her happy and excited, without any negative experiences or bad feelings attached. She marked this door with a red ☺ mark.

     Poppy thought she had found the perfect way to experience multiple experiences and it was behind this one door. The Mask Room where there are hundreds of masks of different colors, shapes and sizes, with experiences to match. They are displayed on invisible walls. She can see the masks front and back. She did not see any means to hold them up. It looks as if they are floating in air. There is a maze of fairly large rooms. She saw that the masks in each room had plenty of distance between and around all of them. When she walks around each mask, she can see a 10-20 second video style preview, on the inside of each mask, explaining what the mask experience will feel like or reveal. Some of the masks can even alter personalities. Even giving the wearer special powers. This is how she can experience things she normally would not be able to experience. Some of the masks she tried on were positive and an enlightening experience. The danger is that some evil masks can alter the wearer's personality. Some masks will even try to deceive her with the video clip they show. The mask video clip on the back must always be watched to the very end. The evil masks do not reveal their evil until the end of the clip. Poppy has always been very careful to try on only the positive mask's. Most of her encounters are light hearted and uplifting. She always feels inspired and energized after her experiences. She was about to experience another flying mask that had only the wind under her for lift. When she viewed the entire clip to the end and realizing it would not be a positive experience. So she watched another masks clip to the end and enjoyed that masks fast pace flying experience instead. It was very exhilarating. Whatever sport she can imagine and some she can't were available and can be experienced in this room by just putting on a mask. Poppy enjoyed the risk taking of exotic experiences. One mask she tried on was of flying with colorful birds of different sizes and colors. Imagine hundreds of bright colored macaws, parrots and toucans. Poppy felt like one of the flock when she flew with them. Telepathically being of one mind and one movement. Swooping, flying and floating on the air currents. Close flight but never bumping other birds. It was very fast paced and exhilarating. Getting literally a bird's eye view, which means greatly enhanced and acute vision. Similar to a camera zoom lens. The zoom ability gave her a new and unique experience.

There are so many different kinds of masks it is hard for her to choose. The beetle mask gave her the feeling of being a small tiny insect, with the perspective of her surroundings being huge. It was very eye opening for her. Since even small pebbles seemed like skyscrapers or mountains, she did not really like that mask but she was curious and she tried it on. It was not evil but not a real pleasant experience either. It made her feel insignificant and she did not like that feeling.

There are several animal masks she can try on. From cats and dogs to large elephants and rhinos. There was also a fish category. Masks from small aquarium size fish to the largest whale shark. All masks give Poppy the animal and creatures perspective on all of their life experiences. Some are very graphic and uncomfortable.

The animal mask she enjoyed the most was of a giraffe. It gave her the best and highest perspective of the terrain. Poppy did not like the leaf eating part of the experience and usually tried to take off the mask just before it got to the eating part. That was the case for most of the fish and animal masks. Since Poppy only eats fruits and vegetables, she does not like the animal's taste of leaves, raw meat or fish, especially the whale shark eating krill. It is so salty and icky for her. All the experiences are so real.

Poppy was tired of keeping secrets and telling lies to her friends and family. She wanted, no she needed to, confide in someone. She wanted to share these extraordinary experiences with a friend, like Iris. Poppy has known her for about fifty years. Plus, Iris was always curious about what Poppy was doing. Always asking her why she never had time for friends anymore. Poppy finally wore down and was thinking, it might be nice to share these secrets with Iris. She knew it had to be a Liveling she would trust with literally her life. No one else could experience or understand it other than a Liveling, for security and entrance/exit reasons. It was a very serious concern. She finally pulled Iris aside one day, they were at a community meeting when she finally told her. Iris's

reaction was excitement at first and then she was upset that
Poppy could not confide in her earlier. That she did not trust
her enough to tell her before now. They got past this
awkwardness rather quickly. They started exploring all the
rooms Poppy had visited in the past 20 years. Doors that Poppy
knew were positive ones. This went well for a couple months.
Iris was eager to try everything. She especially liked the door
that had the masks. She always wanted to return to the mask
door time after time. It was very addictive to Iris. She kept
wanting more and more. It was really an obsession with her.
There were so many different experiences in that one room
alone. Iris told Poppy her experiences were so real and
exciting. During a special moment of trying on masks with
Poppy, Iris was also having a positive experience with another
mask but she was getting bored. It was a mask she had
experienced many times before. Poppy was relaxed and just
going with the flow of her mask and was unaware of what was
happening to her friend. Iris got tired of only using the ones
Poppy told her she could use. So Iris went to another mask and
quickly watched a clip. It had little fairies that looked harmless.
Iris loved everything fairies. She however did not watch the
entire preview clip. Impulsively she popped it on her face. For
the first two minutes she had a wonderful experience, watching
fairies dance in a dark green meadow with flowers, even moss
hanging from the trees. Iris was getting ready to join the fairies
in dance. Then it happened. So fast, she did not know what hit
her. The fairies turned into evil Trolls and were trying to catch
her. (Some masks can change the wearer's behavior). It was
like she was possessed. Iris felt the power of evil taking over
her. She even started to shoot sparks out of her hands in the
room, literally. She had all the symptoms and the magical
powers that the mask possessed. Some evil masks have found a
way to influence other masks & users. Poppy was enjoying an
experience of cute animals doing tricks and she was laughing.
It was like watching one of those animal videos online, where
they do funny tricks or behaviors that make you laugh out loud.
Then all of a sudden, the cute little animals turned into little
red evil creatures. Pointed tails and ears. Long needle sharp

teeth. Seeing these teeth snapping at her was not a pleasant feeling. More like what nightmares are made of and it was a traumatic experience. At the same time all the leaves started turning brown and shriveling. Poppy immediately took the mask off, before it got a hold of her mind. She was very intuitive like that. She was lucky. Had she left it on for much longer it would not have been possible for Poppy to remove her mask or Iris's. They both would have been on a demonic rampage. Fortunately Poppy was able to remove hers and also grab the mask off Iris. This nullified the evil immediately. The evil masks in the past were partly responsible for the extermination of many clans and many of the Livelings. All perpetuated by a warring clan with evil intentions. Poppy and Iris agreed they should destroy the mask. Remembering scary fire pit tales they both quickly got hammers. Coming down hard on the mask, with a crash. Both watched as it shattered into hundreds of little shards. The reason they smashed it was, so it could not be used by anyone else for evil ulterior motives. They could still see movement in the mask pieces. It was very creepy so they took all the pieces for disposal to the Garbage Room. Using the pull down door option was the safest way to dispose of small things. It went into oblivion. Never to be seen again. If they had thrown the mask pieces into a human garbage can someone could have pulled the pieces out and reassembled them. Sounds slight but the risk was too great. So they agreed this was the best way to disposed of the mask. Or was it?

They decided to leave the Cave of Doors and go back to the main part of Poppy's house to freshen up in a room off the kitchen. This is a huge living room with a natural rock pool. It has the look of a private mini lake in a secluded area. The dressing room is very close to the pool and behind some live bushes. Camouflaging the entrance as not to detract from the outdoor pool/lake area. They discussed the evil event and how they needed to be more vigilant in not rushing to use a mask or anything behind any door, without first researching whether it is good or evil. This is a life and death decision with the doors-rooms use. Discussing this while they were lounging on the smooth rock shoreline after they had such a traumatic experience they were unable to relax. That is when Poppy took Iris to her private door-room and introduced her to what she had created from scratch.

As soon as they entered, Iris turned to Poppy and said she wanted to create a room of her own. One she could design anyway she wanted to get her mind off the scary mask incident. Poppy said yes and immediately started helping her. The design was similar to her own private room that she goes to for relaxation and to reflect on issues. In Poppy's special room she has a Caribbean style bungalow. Full of rattan furniture, aqua blue water in the background surrounding a pink sandy beach. For Iris she even added a cool tropical breeze. Iris wanted to add a patch of emerald green grass with flowers framing it. Taller ferns and palm trees in the background. They added multicolored butterflies flying about and some Dolphin like creatures, who swam up to the beach and motioned for Iris and Poppy to join them. Nodding their heads several times, like a horse does, this is just what they needed, after the bad experience they had just gone through. Iris joined the dolphin creatures in the water. They offered her and Poppy a ride on their backs. Poppy joined her on another dolphin creature's back. They swam under the water and jumped high into the air. Poppy also created a fish type creature for Iris, similar to the Sea Horse. She made them very large, about 6 to 8 feet long, large enough to ride. Iris wanted the realism and detail of the human world. But she wanted the exaggerated size and colors. These seahorses were bright yellow with red colored bows on their back spine. They were not able to jump as high as the dolphin creatures. They did enjoy seeing them swimming alongside. When riding the Seahorses it was to slow and not as exciting. Much better for long conversations. They only rode them when they wanted to relax, go slow and talk. Dolphins were more exhilarating to ride and helped Iris and Poppy forget all that had happened. It was similar to the experience of riding a horse, but in the water. It is so much smoother and faster than anyone can ride a horse. Together they created different colors and types. One is similar to a Leafy Sea Dragon, after creating them. Iris did not like riding them because they have too much ornamental leafy seaweed skin. It gets in the way and makes it harder to see around or maneuver. She did not want to pull or make it uncomfortable for the seahorse or rider. The regular Sea Horse creatures were easiest to just jump on and go for a slow ride. Iris kept the Seahorse Dragons because they were so pretty to look at, while they were swimming around the beach area or alongside. Their coloring was green and blue hues with purple accents. Iris and Poppy rode the dolphins for a couple more hours. Iris finally grew tired and decided to lay on her new beach for a while. The nice thing about the pink sand they created is that it did not stick to them, like real sand. It just falls off. Not even one piece sticks to their skin. No need to create beach towels or blankets. It was awesome. Very relaxing and enjoyable. When they get hungry, they enjoy walking over and picking fruit from the trees that were created near the emerald green grass. The fruit is very colorful. Bright vivid reds, pinks, purple, yellow and extremely flavorful. They can eat the whole fruit, so no waste or mess. There are no seeds or tough outer skin. The fruit flavors they created are a combination of pineapple/cherry and peach/strawberry. Both are yummy flavors. Iris's favorite is the peach/strawberry but Poppy's was the pineapple/cherry. Drinking water is plentiful from the spring that runs behind and around the Palm trees. Iris can change the flow or any other architecture, just by letting Poppy know what she wants to change. Iris did not have the ability to make changes on her own. This is the process of how all the rooms were formed. It is part Liveling imagination and part magic of the caves. This gift was only endowed to a few Livelings in history and Poppy had the real gift of creation.

The reason some evil rooms were created is because of a few rare evil Liveling's in the past. They had evil thoughts and created the evil masks and doors to do their bidding. Whoever put on these masks became consumed by its evil. It affected others wearing masks in a close proximity to the evil mask wearer. Some clans were never heard from again. There are several conflicting stories. Poppy is not sure what the actual facts are. The fire pit stories said they disappeared into the masks. No one really knows. Another possible reason the populations were almost wiped out forever. So the doors were deemed off limits, magically hidden from sight and ordered forbidden. There are a lot of very positive masks and doors that are used for only good experiences. Dangerous or evil masks and doors could not be allowed. Such an evil force could be used for the possibility of turning all mask wearers evil eventually. Poppy had rules to prevent this from happening. Occasionally mistakes happen to the unaware. It is not always evil intentions. That is why Poppy and Iris created and needed an outlet room to recuperate from the rare bad experiences like this. This does not solve the evil mask or door problem though. It only helps with their immediate mental healing. They will have to address this problem again someday, so it does not happen again and the possibility of wiping out the Livelings very existence.

For anyone who loves stories of cute delicate Fairies, the Fairy room would be ideal. Poppy has not shared this door with Iris. It is a very personal door for her, because of her experiences with the Royal Fairy family. When Poppy walked through the door for the first time she was surrounded by a lush green meadow that had an atmosphere of bustling springs running through this meadow with beautiful low growing flowers surrounding small ponds of many colors, even some colors outside of the human spectrum of vision. It looked like a painting. It is so perfect. Not a brown leaf or blade of grass. Consistent with all the other positive rooms. Dancing around the meadow were Fairies and not your ordinary run of the mill Fairies. They were translucent, light and delicate. She was barely able to see them unless they wanted to be seen. When the Royal Family allowed Poppy to see them she immediately saw all of them from then on. The Fairies are actually very dainty, energetic and intelligent. They have sparkly, colored faces. It is mesmerizing to watch them dance, twirl and float about the meadow so gracefully. When they are not dancing and flittering about they are taking care of the meadow plants, flowers and animals. It truly is awesome to watch. It gives Poppy a relaxed feeling and yet it sparks her visual senses and she consciously tries to drink in more and more color. It is so visually pleasant and stimulating. It is almost hypnotic. She spends a lot of time in this room, especially since she has become friends with so many of the fairies and even the Royal Fairy family. It is a very rare and a high honor indeed. Some of the fairies have never even personally met the royal family. When Poppy met them it was special. They even had a royal ceremony, honoring Poppy and her friendship with the fairies. They rolled out the royal purple and red carpet and a path lined with flowers. They also had flower covered trellis's that had several small, real rainbows in between them. The rainbows went from one side, overhead about eight foot in the air and attaching to the ground on the other side of the royal carpet, leading to the royal fairy throne. Poppy was amazed at the colors in the rainbows used in this ceremony. Especially having rainbows you can walk under. She walked slowly under each one to visually drink it all in, all the way to the throne. She felt very special. This was one of her favorite experiences. The throne was tiny as you would expect. About 10 inches high. Being tiny, did not make it any less impressive. It is made of solid gold, with a very strong, fine invisible fairy thread, holding precious gem stones in place that adorn the top and sides of this royal throne. Intricate patterns are carved into the gold. Scenes of Fairies flying over the plants and animals that they protect and take care of. Poppy has to lean in close to see all the beautiful detailed pictures carved into the throne. After she went under the last rainbow arch, she met the Royal Couple and they all bowed to each other, showing respect.

The ceremony was very moving for Poppy. She watched and witnessed all the Fairies, birds and animals, standing almost at attention. Not flittering about in the air, but standing on the ground or in the trees. This was to show respect for the Royal Fairy Family and Poppy. She was representing the Liveling's. Poppy was in awe, when she saw all the birds and animals that came from deep in the forest. She had seen some of them come to the Livelings for treatment of serious injuries before. But never had she seen them come together for an event in a room. Especially one like this that honored her friendship with the Royal Fairy Family. Poppy could telepathically feel the love and admiration. She was not sure how it was possible to see some of these animals and fairies in her world and in this door-world too, since only Liveling's can enter or exit. It is a question for later. It is mind boggling. Poppy made a mental note to bring this up with the Fairies at a different time. For right now she wanted to drink in all the pomp and circumstance. It was an amazing sight to see. All the spectators were sharing and not fighting for space. Small animals, rabbits and chipmunks were sitting on larger animals. The larger animals were allowing the smaller ones to sit on their backs and antlers, so all could have a better view of the festivities. News carried quickly throughout this world. Tree limbs were crowded with birds and squirrels all sharing limb space. You would think it would be overwhelming but it was exciting and awe inspiring at the same time. Poppy enjoyed all the celebrations. Even the party after the ceremony, lasting for hours. Her energy level remained high and energized because of the positive output of love.

On another day and behind another door, Poppy called this one her in The Water Room. When she opens this door, she can see what appears to be a Plexiglas type barrier or force field, which is holding the water back and completely covering the door from top to bottom. She can see fish and creatures swimming by as if in an aquarium. She would sometimes just open the door and view it like an aquarium. The barrier is flat and smooth. She can observe the fish swimming by and it is very therapeutic. Her friend, Ralph, the Beatnik Jellyfish, would usually show up. They would always have an interesting conversation. He did not have fingers to snap, like a Beatnik, so when he agreed with her, he would rub his tentacles together in a manner that it had a similar sound. On occasions she would step inside and it is like magic. She never feels cramped or claustrophobic. The fish always surround her in a welcoming stature and it looks like they are always smiling. It is always a very positive experience and never intimidating. Poppy would just step in thru the door and immediately she was able to breath. The world is filled with friendly, unique fish and other sea creatures. Being in the water and able to breath was a very odd feeling. When she moved it felt like, what you would imagine walking on the moon is like. She just bent her knees to lift off. She could float and direct her movement with her arms or legs. Similar to swimming only easier. There did not seem to be any noticeable resistance. She did detect a slight current. It always seemed to be going the way she wanted. It made getting around a lot easier than she thought it would be. Poppy interacted with all the friendly fish and even the sharks. Sharks are the friendliest of all the water creatures in this world. They help all the other fish, shellfish and crabs when they have a problem. Sharks are like a big brother to the smaller, frailer fish or shrimp. Not that there are any serious problems, but if one of them gets stuck or trapped behind something that is too heavy. The sharks are always ready and willing to help move the obstruction and do it with a smile. These sharks are very polite and always use proper etiquette. They always say please and thank you. Yes, all the fish, crabs and other small creatures can talk. The Sharks dispositions are comparable to fine English gentlemen in their tuxedos. Quite the opposite of what you would expect from a shark. Sharks have gotten a bum rap and in this water world they more than make up for it. Poppy's favorite shark friends name is Bob. Poppy has become very close friends with Bob.

Shark colors are different. Not the normal colors you would expect. No drab grays or browns in here. All the Sharks colors are bright red with yellow and orange tipped gills. Bob looks like he is on fire when he moves quickly in the currents. The fact that Poppy has red hair with yellow and orange highlights is perhaps why she feels close to the sharks. Possibly because of their color similarity they share. All the fish are vibrant bright colors. There are also electric green eels and even blue type turtle creatures. These are just to name a few. Poppy often visits Bob to attend his version of an English Afternoon Tea along with all the pomp and circumstance that would go with an afternoon tea time experience. Pinky finger and fin in the air too. There is no eating of one another in this world. All food is provided. It just keeps regenerating and no creature big or small wants for anything, except for the occasional help from the sharks. It is perfect. No illness, hunger and no abnormalities. Only the unusual color schemes. All the creatures and fish are all perfectly healthy and live long fulfilling lives. In fact she thinks they all live forever like the Livelings. She never sees any of them die. That is a question she has not asked, because it would be impolite to ask as well as asking their ages.

There appears to be no visible signs of bubbles not even coming from Poppy. She is also not sure how it works, but it does. She is not even sure how far back this world goes or how big it is. She has never seen another side. It seems to go on forever and she has never asked. There are large creatures that look similar to Turtles and Rays. They help with long distance transportation for the smaller fish and creatures, including shrimp and small crabs that cannot move over great distances quickly. In payment, they help by removing the rare algae build up. They clean all the little cracks and crevices. It is like a mini massage for the turtles and rays, which makes for a pleasurable and uplifting journey. Poppy was told they travel to group meetings or ceremonies from time to time. There is no negativity and everyone gets along and helps each other. It is a lesson that could be learned by many in the human world. They

often break out in song just like you would expect in some of
the cartoon aquatic movies. It is so much fun to watch and
absorb all that is going on. Poppy can spend hours in this world
and never see all that is happening. Parades of beautiful
multicolored fish, move past her so gracefully. Some of their
tails and fins look like feather plumes dancing as if blowing in
the wind, as they swim by. She can hear the clicking of the
crab claws, as though they are playing castanets, keeping time
to the music that felt like it surrounds and enveloped all. There
is never a dull moment in this room. It is one big happy party.

Another one of Poppy and Iris's favorite doors is the
Flying Room. They can fly by just jumping up. They are able
to fly free. No wings required. They have experienced having
wings, from a mask room. It was not a pleasurable experience
for them. It was stressful and they were always conscious of
how they needed to keep flapping their arms or they felt like
they would fall out of the sky. This mask flying experience
without wings, they were able to soar over the terrain with only
their arms out. They could see everything best from 10 to 100
foot up in the air. They never really tried to fly higher. It was
truly more exhilarating the closer they were to the terrain,
following the contours while swooping and diving on the air
currents. They can also see the animals and plant life better
when up close. Some of the terrain was rolling hills covered
with emerald green low growing bushes. No tall trees in this
world to fly into. Inter mixed are magenta colored daisy type
flowers. These flowers have little faces in the center of their
petals. Lovely red lips and twinkly blue eyes. In another
meadow there is a pansy style flower with yellow and purple
petals around cute little faces. Including the pansy, black
accent marks. That look like whiskers and creating personality
to their little faces. All the flowers have separate personalities.
Simply wrinkling their face creates expressions when swaying
in the wind. Moving as if they are all listening to the same
music. All Poppy could hear was the wind as she flew over
them. The ground animals were all cute, small and more rodent
sized, so not intimidating. She watched them running and

jumping, as if they wanted her to race with them. No birds in this world to collide with so they did not have to worry. She actually enjoyed flying through the occasional low cloud. It was a brisk encounter that was over quickly, since the clouds are very small, fluffy and white. More of a mist and never any dark clouds. Poppy has visited this door several times before. Each time she visits the colors and ground cover had changed. There might be a different color or leaf shape or maybe a wider leaf and a darker green. Sometimes a more slender and feathery thin leaf. The flowers may be pink verses the purple that they were before. There are even flowers that are sometimes rainbow colors and stripes. It is exciting for Poppy and Iris to see what changes there might be on their next visit.

They can fly as slow or as fast as they wanted. To go slow they would just give a light push off or if already flying they could open their arms and legs to slow down. If they wanted to go faster, they would get a running start, if already flying they can also close their arms to their sides, to pick up speed. If they wanted to moderate the pace they would open their arms, for resistance. They enjoyed fast and slow flight for different reasons. Each gave them a new perspective. When they fly low there are so many details that they miss when flying fast and high. They enjoyed both, especially with the ever changing landscape.

They had to set up a light beacon that could be seen from a great distance in case they went too far. This way they could find their way back to the exit. They needed a beam of light that shone hundreds of feet in the air. For the day time Poppy created a blinking light. It is very bright and shone even on a sunny day. It has a metallic backing and the light bounces off of it. These are very important additions so they could find the door opening and get back to the exit. Each visit for them always had different and new creatures and landscape changes. It made it more exciting since it was never the same twice. They are not sure how it changes but happy it did. So, it was

not really necessary to venture further than before to find
something different.

Poppy and Iris have never experienced snow like this
next room. The snow temperature adjusts from cold to warm.
The snow never melts and it does not get dirty. It is always
perfect. Each snowflake is large and easy to see the perfection.
Beautiful one of a kind designs and a master piece each one.
Poppy can even change them to a different color of the
spectrum. Sometimes even black which is very unusual indeed.
When the snow is black the landscape usually is in florescent
shades of darker more vibrant colors. The shapes on the ground
that the snowflakes cover can be altered by Poppy. Depending
on her moods or if Iris asks her to change them, they
sometimes like trees with soft edges and other times possibly
triangles, squares or multiple ridged forms, for the snow to fall
on. Poppy can change all of this and more, just by thinking of a
color or shape. Even the background colors of the sky and
clouds. Mentally for her it is the same as the exercise of
working on a puzzle.

It is very relaxing for them to watch the snow fall
gently and feel the snowflakes landing on their faces and
tongues. They could see the snow blowing in a movement that
was almost musical in nature. It moves and swirls as if to
music. When Poppy wants to get trick, she can even change
the taste of these snowflakes, depending on her mood. It could
taste like chocolate, fruity or she even tried a three course meal
one time. It did not work well. She lost concentration and did
not even get through the second course. Plus who wants snow
to taste like a steak or potato? All she has to do is think of a
flavor and voila. The snowflake takes on that flavor and color.

In this snow world there is a perfect brick path, Poppy
and Iris can walk on. It is always clean, like someone has just
swept it. There are no wet shoes or slush to deal with and the
snow does not gather on this special path. There are also
colorful birds flying about. They are always cheerful and

singing beautiful songs. They are not hibernating or hiding
from horrible cold temperatures that normally goes with snow.
No doom and gloom anywhere in this world. In some areas
there are even flowers blooming. Such a pretty contrast. It is so
gorgeous, words cannot even describe it. When Poppy is in her
mountain home and sees a meadow with snow on it, she
remembers how it sparkles in the sun and looks like someone
sprinkled it with diamonds. Now imagine a marble type pattern
to this snow. In addition there are beautiful shades of purple,
pink or red. When these vibrant colors blend with the white
snow and the flowers peeking through, it is spectacular. With
multiple color variances, it is even more beautiful than you can
ever imagine. It gives you a feeling of what God really had in
mind.

The Floor World door leads to a large room
approximately 100 foot x 150 foot. Past the door is a really
dark blue floor. The color of a deep ocean. The floor feels and
looks like walking on a one inch gel. As Poppy walks, she
leaves a footprint. The print appears immediately and in
seconds would disappear. The depth of her foot print is about
one eight inch deep. When she walks across the floor it felt
cool on her bare feet and she could see that there is an actual
ocean world below the surface. Poppy enjoyed walking on this
gel floor barefoot. That way she could experience the cool
squish. It appears life is going on with business as usual, even
as she walks on it and there is no effect on this world at all. It
would be the same as walking on her world clouds and there
would not be a noticeable indentation. She can see tiny
Schooner ships cruising across the water. Large, but tiny in
comparison to her world. Sea creatures that look like they are
part Dragon and part Eel, swimming in the water. They look
like ribbons with several sections in and out of the water at the

same time. Towering over this miniature world made Poppy feel like a giant.

At the far side of the room, there are couches she can relax in. She can sit on a couch and looks down at the floor in front of her. She observes several different sized television type screens, inside the gel floor. Poppy is also able to walk on this extension of the water world as well. It reacts the same as the water side. So, it did not interfere with the screens. The screens are playing different programs like the weather channel, sports, news and movies from the human world. She just needed to think of a subject and the screens would switch channels. She can also adjust the sound by thought. This is how she kept tabs on current events.

The "Frozen in Time" room is another room that is in a folk tale of lost Liveling's that were never to be heard from again. Poppy made this room her challenge and goal to bring back the lost souls who met with this unfortunate door. The biggest issue on the other side of this door is different for everyone who opens it. Some envisioned their living room, others would see anything from a meadow and waterfall to the inside of a rock. That is why it is so treacherous. They are sucked into familiar surroundings and once in, they are transported to only they know where. The destination is based on thought and whatever popped into their mind. So, if the Liveling unfortunately thinks of something bad or a time long past, it can have serious consequences. No one has ever come back to tell their story. Poppy wanted to share these experiences with more than just Iris and did not want to hide anymore. But she had to be cautious and only tell Iris for now. Poppy believed all the doors with issues had to be identified and locked to protect the curious and future generations. Someday she will devise a way to either bring the lost back or go out and rescue them. Not sure at this time how she will do that. One time she tried by tying a rope around her waist and that did not work. She almost experienced the same fate. The only thing that saved her was a dust cleaning broom that

swooped past her to get a speck of dust and vanished before
her eyes. That is how she was saved. Other Liveling's were not
so lucky. Realizing she could get lost forever or die, she racked
her brain trying to think of other rescue methods. Poppy is
smart and can usually figure out problems quickly. She was not
going to give up hope and knew she would need more planning
and more testing before she was ready to try it herself. She
remembered the Liveling rule was in effect and no inanimate
object could be used. Trying a teapot, the rope it was attached
to was severed. It had to be a Liveling to save a Liveling.
Poppy is not a quitter and will not give up and will continue to
research until she finds a way. She always runs scenarios by
the friendly dragon Sordo for advice. But since the door deals
with an altered reality and time travel he cannot help her.
Sordo can usually help with other type of circumstances. He
asked her to give him time to ponder since, it is a difficult
problem. He has a great sense of what would or would not
work and he has been proven over and over again to be
accurate in other scenarios. Even if Sordo cannot come up with
the correct or ideal way to save the lost Liveling's or how to
enter safely to find them. They have just disappeared. Right
now that is all they have to go on. There are not really any
facts to show that they even used this door. With no real
information and her almost ending up with a horrible fate. She
will never give up the search and trying to figure out what
happened to them and how to bring them back, safely if
possible. For now she must move on and abandon thoughts of
bringing them back.

Iris and Poppy enjoyed the magic doors and rooms for
years with nothing major going wrong. They came up with
checks and balances. This went on for decades and than Iris for
some reason got careless. She forgot the golden rule. Never
talk to others about their adventures. One night she had too
much Dandelion Wine by the fire pit. Their secret life popped
out and the Livelings sitting close to Iris asked her to explain.
She spilled the beans and broke the sacred trust she had
maintained for so many years with Poppy. Poppy was not at

this party. So, she was unable to stop Iris from continuing to tell all that they have done and in great detail. Iris exposed how they were able to experience these adventures. She even mentioned they were trying to bring back the lost Liveling's and more.

Iris was out of control in her nonchalant betrayal. She had even mentioned that she has started to visit different doors without Poppy. Poppy unaware of her deceit and hearing of it for the first time from others, she was furious. One of the rooms Iris talked about visiting without Poppy was an unusual room of ever changing furniture. It looked like a furniture store with aisles and rows of furniture. Iris was shopping for new and upgraded furniture. She was bored with her ho-hum existence and wanted more luxury in her life. Mentioning the aisles were not like normal furniture store aisles. They were ever changing and sometimes never ending, filled with unique furniture like you have never seen. Some items are larger than normal, with incredible patterns and vibrant colors. Just to give you an idea, one huge couch looked like it was made of red leather that was melting and dripping over several levels. It looked like a shallow stream running down a mountainside with multiple mini waterfalls flowing over rocks. But, it actually looked good. The further Iris went into the room the more it changed. Furniture colors became even more vibrant and colorful. Just standing and looking out across the room. She said it looked like walls of color strips that you would see when entering a paint store. With multiple shades of the same color and style. No basic beige or dull browns. But hundreds of different shades of purples, blues, reds, yellow, teals, etc. and they were all so bright. However, she could not appreciate the beauty of the furniture since it became more evil in its intent the further in she went. The floors turned into water and the further in the room the higher the water got. Soon there were small Barracuda like creatures in the water. Iris found herself running to get out of the water and jumped on to some of the furniture, to find safety, only to find the furniture was evil too. Iris jumping from chairs to couches she noticed the furniture with the animated faces were chasing her too. The evil furniture colors were darker reds and black. They looked demonic. Iris thought if she ran fast enough she could finally get to another room that would be normal. But then it would change, as soon as she got further inside. In another room there were doll like beings trying to catch her. While still running past brilliant colors and fabulous looking furniture. In another room the aisles narrowed and there were dog like creatures chasing her. One of the creatures was hurt and disfigured. It seemed to understand telepathically that if it was willing to help Iris get out. Iris was willing to help and take it out the exit doorway with her. This happened in an instantaneous thought. Iris continued into an accessory area with colorful glass sculptures mixed in with inanimate, unthreatening couches. They were all very ultra- modern in design, color and texture. Many were unique; like nothing she had ever seen. She really could not doddle to shop due to the creatures chasing her. She kept trying to escape whatever was in that area. Suddenly she remembered only Liveling's can access the doors. But she did not let the creature know that she had a revelation. When Iris finally got to the exit with the creatures help, she pretended to try and take the creature out. After it had performed admirably in keeping the evil things from catching Iris, by tricking them to follow it instead of Iris. This is the only reason Iris escaped. The magic barrier was still working though. Iris then exited and the injured dog like creature could not. She had to explain the harsh truth to it in a quick thought. Understanding, it coward off and hid behind an oversized couch that was not evil. Iris never knew what happened to the poor creature that helped her. She dashed out of the exit quickly and never looked back. She was glad to be alive. She never went into that door again and never even made an effort to think of how she could help that poor creature.

Poppy was so excited about having a friend to experience adventures with. She had set up a door that linked both her homes because it made it easier for her friend, Iris did not have the ability to teleport and since the Cave of Doors were hidden from view, Iris needed a way in. That is where Poppies fears became a reality. Her worst fear came true. The day after Iris had too much Dandelion Wine, they were exposed. Iris was hungover and careless. She was not paying attention to her surroundings the day after and Iris exposed their secret. Not realizing she was being followed by a Youngling, his named Bug, short for Bugsy. He was only 45 years old, which is young for a Liveling. He is very curious and is always getting into trouble. He had a fascination with Iris and would follow her without her knowing. Bugs overheard Iris when she unexpectedly told the story of all the adventures they had in the Cave of Doors. Well, he followed her to the secret door. The door Poppy had created for Iris. After Iris walked through the door she never looked back to verify it had closed. This was so careless because Bug was able to grab the door, just as it was getting ready to latch closed. He pulled on it quickly and to his amazement it opened quite easily. It was a heavy looking rock design, so it would blend in better with the mountain walls. There was a secret panel that Iris needed to enter in a secret code. The panel to unlock the door was hidden by plants. Iris just needed to push them aside so she could enter the code. After the code was entered the plants would fall back into place and hide the panel again. Only then would the door unlock. Now, Bug had learned the secret. What would this mean? Would this secret get out to the rest of the Liveling's or even the humans? This could be the end of the whole Liveling existence. Or was it?

The End